Beyond the Palace Walls

By ALEXANDRA LAZAR

Screenplay by JOHN AUGUST and GUY RITCHIE
Based on Disney's *ALADDIN*

DISNEP PRESS

LOS ANGELES • NEW YORK

$\mathcal{T}$his is the story of Princess Jasmine. Her father was the Sultan. He ruled a kingdom called Agrabah. Jasmine wanted to become sultana someday.

But she knew she needed to see the kingdom outside the palace.

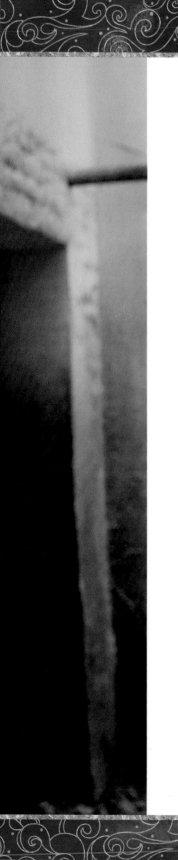

Jasmine snuck out of the palace to the marketplace. She saw children who looked hungry. She wanted to help them. So she gave them bread.

A merchant named Jamal thought the disguised Jasmine was stealing. He called the guards.

A young man named Aladdin saw Jasmine getting in trouble. Aladdin was a thief, but he had a kind heart.

Aladdin decided to help. He tricked Jamal with the help of his pet monkey, Abu.

Jasmine was able to escape while Jamal was distracted.

Together, Jasmine and Aladdin ran away from the guards. Aladdin knew how to outsmart them.

Jasmine and Aladdin leaped onto a rooftop. The guards could not follow them.

Then Aladdin took Jasmine to his hideout. He lived in an old tower near the marketplace.

Aladdin didn't know that
Jasmine was a princess.
He liked her for her clever
mind and caring heart.
He recognized what made
Jasmine special.

Jasmine was kind. She wanted to help the people of Agrabah.

She filled her bedroom with books and maps. Jasmine was smart. She studied every day to learn more about the world around her.

Jasmine knew she could make life better
for her people.

But her father expected her to marry a
prince instead.

Countless suitors wanted to marry Jasmine for her wealth and beauty. But none of them noticed that she was smart and kind. They only cared that she was a beautiful princess.

Jasmine didn't like any of the princes. Raja, her pet tiger, didn't like them, either.

Jasmine knew that she was the best leader for Agrabah. No one cared about its people more than she did.

She wanted to visit other parts of the kingdom to meet her people and learn about their lives.

Jasmine read and learned.
She worked to understand
Agrabah and its people.

She knew that Agrabah
needed her.

Jasmine's kindness and compassion made her a perfect princess. They would make her an even better leader.

Jasmine would not give up on her dream of leading Agrabah.

Jasmine was confident in herself. But she ran into obstacles. Her father wanted to protect her.

His advisor, Jafar, wanted to control her. She needed to find a way to make her dreams come true.

Jasmine's friends believed in her. Raja
supported her. And her handmaiden,
Dalia, was with her every step of the way.